CALGARY PUBLIC LIBRARY

JAN / / 2003

Jeoffry's Halloween

MARY BRYANT BAILEY

PICTURES BY **ELIZABETH SAYLES**

FARRAR STRAUS GIROUX · *NEW YORK*

Text copyright © 2003 by Mary Bryant Bailey
Illustrations copyright © 2003 by Elizabeth Sayles
All rights reserved
Distributed in Canada by Douglas & McIntyre Ltd.
Color separations by Prime Digital Media
Printed and bound in the United States of America by Berryville Graphics
Typography by Nancy Goldenberg
First edition, 2003
1 3 5 7 9 10 8 6 4 2

Library of Congress Cataloging-in-Publication Data
Bailey, Mary Bryant.
    Jeoffry's Halloween / Mary Bryant Bailey ; pictures by Elizabeth Sayles.— 1st ed.
      p.   cm.
    Summary: After roaming through fields, woods, and streets on Halloween night,
Jeoffry the cat is glad to finally return home.
    ISBN 0-374-33677-6
    [1. Halloween—Fiction.   2. Cats—Fiction.   3. Stories in rhyme.]   I. Sayles,
Elizabeth, ill.   II. Title.

PZ8.3.B153 Ji 2002
[E]—dc21

                                                                              2002022822

Glossary

bog: wet, muddy ground; a wetland
copse: a small group of trees
dale: a valley
lichen: a crusty, slow-growing plant found on rocks and trees
shock: a bundle of cornstalks arranged in a tepee shape for drying
tupelo: a tree that grows in swampy places and sometimes in groves;
also called a beetlebung

To my father, Nelson Bryant, and my
mother, Jean Morgan Bryant, who
gave me their love for words
                    —MBB

For Pouncer, Isabel, and the Cats
on the Roof
                    —ES

In Autumn, when the garden's worn,
I hide and seek in shocks of corn.
While leaves burst into flames of red,
the sleepy scarecrow hangs its head.
Crowns of yawning sunflowers droop.
Down to their seeds the finches swoop.

The hound's howl calls me through the haze
to the garden, where pumpkins blaze.
As frost has not yet laced the straw,
the warm sod sinks beneath our paws.
We creep to where fat bullfrogs croak
and lichens shawl the gnarly oak.

I hear the panting of the dog
where stillness haunts the swirling bog.
Ghostly wings beat in the mist
and surround us with a hiss.
The dog's tail wags when he sees
familiar shapes of huddled geese.

Darkness glides along the hills;
into the dales it swiftly spills.
We peek above the old stone wall
at bristly bandits in a brawl:
two raccoons who choose the night
to roam about and pick a fight.

A whisper, as the farmer's gate's unhitched—
It's a Goblin and a Witch!

The frightened dog runs in the house.
I, as silent as a mouse,
follow the two along the street,
as they holler, "Trick or treat!"
A wailing horde of hollow hoods
scares the pair into the woods.

Ghouls glide round the prickly tops
of beeches twinkling in a copse.
They're only squirrels flying by,
dropping nutshells from the sky.
Still, the Witch and Goblin shriek!
Their flashlight falls into the creek.

We're in a grove of tupelos;
dark creatures watch us pass below.
We wander through thickets of fright,
whose claws reach out into the night!
I'll be the Witch and Goblin's scout
and find a way to lead them out.

A somber cloud puts out a star.
We hear a rumble from afar.
A dragon blows fire at the sky;
the brilliance makes a rooster cry.
Underneath the lightning's glare
is merely a rambunctious mare.

Fallen stars the Witch has caught.
The Goblin has a clever thought—
fireflies to light the sack!
The lantern finds me in the black.

When they see I'm the farmer's cat,
they take off their masks and hats.

Away from the gloomy woods we roam,
back to the comfort of our homes.
I see the farmer in the corn,
beneath his straw hat, tipped and torn.
A rough wind blows the hat away,
baring the scarecrow's head of hay!

My tail fattens in the chill.
Of Halloween I've had my fill!
It's time to go inside the house,
where a mouse is just a mouse,
where cream is cream, fish is fish,
a dog's a dog, a dish a dish.

The door opens with a creak.

Above, a thing on wing goes "squeak!"

Sometimes, a bat is just a bat.

I'm happy just to be a cat.